Sandy's Been Saved

Ann Edgerton Darling

WestBow Press books may be ordered through booksellers or by contacting:

WestBow Press
A Division of Thomas Nelson & Zondervan
1663 Liberty Drive
Bloomington, IN 47403
www.westbowpress.com
1 (866) 928-1240

ISBN: 978-1-9736-5405-6 (sc)
ISBN: 978-1-9736-5406-3 (e)

Library of Congress Control Number: 2019901882

Print information available on the last page.

WestBow Press rev. date: 3/19/2019

WestBow
PRESS®
A DIVISION OF THOMAS NELSON
& ZONDERVAN

Table of Contents

Chapter 1
DISCOVERY

My name is Dog and this is my story. I live on my own since my family left me when they moved away. I don't know why they didn't want me anymore but I have been so sad and hungry since they left me.

I like to lie in the road to keep warm during the day. Maybe if I stay here, they may come back and get me. The lady that lives next door will give me food every once in a while but she will never let me come into her house. She already has two dogs and I guess she doesn't want another one. She is the one that named me "Dog".

There is a man that has driven by a few times and he always slows down and waves to me. That is pretty strange since not many people will wave at a dog.

I am so sad and feel sick ever since those dogs attacked me a few weeks ago. At night it's hard to find a warm place to sleep but tonight I dug a hole next to the house where my family lived. I will stay warm here tonight and see what happens tomorrow.

During the night something really strange started happening to me. I am having puppies. Somehow I just knew what I had to do and when it was over, I had three little precious babies. How can I take care of them and still have time to search for food?

Just as I was thinking that, I heard the neighbor lady call me. "Dog....Dog!" so I came running. When I got there the man that would wave to me from his car was there. He said, "Come here sweet girl, let me pet you".

I ran as fast as I could back to my babies but he was hot on my trail. When he caught up with me, he said, "Oh you poor baby. You are just a puppy yourself."

He asked the lady, "Do you know where her owners went?" She replied, "They moved away weeks ago and just left the dog here. They had a bunch of kids and I guess they just didn't want to be bothered with a dog too. They asked me if I wanted her but I already have 2 dogs of my own."

"That does it." said man. "I'm going to take them with me right now."

Before I knew it, the adventure had started and my new life was about to begin. It was pretty amazing that he showed up on the very day that I needed him most.

He packed the pups and me into his car and took us to a warm building and gave us all a bath and some delicious food like I had never had before.

"I'm thinking that this might be a good thing," I said to my pups. They didn't understand me yet but I think they were as happy as I was. We were out of that hole and in a safe warm place.

Soon, he was putting us into this little cozy container that was nice and warm. He put us in this small space under a seat and then my ears started popping and wherever we were made a loud roaring noise. It was perfect for a nap, so we all fell sound asleep.

When we awakened man took us out of the container and we were in a real warm place. The sunshine felt so good and everything was really green.

The man took me to his house and there was a lady there with a little dog. Bruiser was his name and he didn't like me at all. He was half my size but he just kept barking and growling at me. I needed to show him who was boss so I jumped on him and started biting. Well, you have never heard so much screaming in all your life.

"Get that dog out of here!" said the lady. "She's vicious. There is no room here for 4 more dogs. She's cute but we can't have her attacking Bruiser like that."

I heard man say, "Honey, this is the dog that I've been telling you about. You know, the one on the road. I found out she had been abandoned and when I saw she had the pups....I just had to save them and fly them back here to Florida." He explained. "Just give me a little time and I will find them all a home.

Later I found out that man was named Karl and he had found us in a place called Oklahoma. It was winter time there and it was very cold but this place called Florida was warm, even in the winter. I was so happy to be in a warm place where my bones never got so cold that they hurt.

I also found out that the lady was Karl's wife and she really was nice but her loyalty was to Bruiser. She helped him find us a temporary home. I guess there really are some nice people in this world. This is turning into quite an adventure.

Chapter 2
MY TEMPORARY HOME

The home that Karl found for us was a wonderful place for my puppies and me. I could feed them and teach them all about being adorable so one day they could be adopted by someone to love them.

Mopsy was the only little girl and she looked the most like me. She was very sweet and patient when her brothers were pushing her out of the way to eat. I could tell that one day she would be a natural mother.

Bootsy was a playful little guy but there was something wrong with his back leg. He managed to get around pretty well using his other 3 legs. That taught him to be very persistent. I think that will help him to be a good and loyal dog and easy to be trained by his new owner. He also had four white paws which is why I called him Bootsy.

Skully was the one that held the group together. He was so gentle and peaceful and nothing seemed to get him too excited. He always seemed to be in control of the situation and would keep the others from going astray.

Since this was not our permanent home our caretakers didn't show us much attention. I think they just didn't want to get attached to us. They fed us and would take us outside once a day. We spent a lot of time together in a play pen and I was starting to feel trapped.

Boy oh boy, did I miss being outside and living on the street. In the old days, I got to do what I wanted when I wanted, with no one to tell me what to do. But it sure was nice now getting regular food and it was also fun having my puppies to keep me company. Living on your own can be pretty lonely.

Many people came to look at us to see if we were what they wanted. Every time the door opened, I would run for it and try to escape. I really wasn't trying to get away from my puppies but I just wanted to be outside and chase the squirrels and these funny little creatures they called lizards.

Most of the people that came were looking at the puppies because not many people wanted a grown up dog like me. I didn't really care because I wanted to be independent and live on my own again.

But one day this nice lady came and she didn't seem at all interested in my puppies but she spent so much time petting and talking to me.

At the end of our visit, she put me on a leash and took me for a walk. No one had ever done this before. It was kind of a pain being hooked to her but at least I got to be outside.

She said goodbye to me and I didn't think I would see her again but about a week later she came back and picked me up and took me in her car to this other house.

There was a man there and he didn't seem real interested in me but I could tell he was just holding back. He called her Ann and she called him sweetie.

"Sweetie, you just need to give her a chance. We need to see if she will warm up to us. Maybe we can see if she likes our backyard."

Well, when she opened the door I was amazed. There were a ton of squirrels and lizards lurking in all the bushes. I stumbled over my front paws trying to get out there quickly.

I had so much fun running free and scurrying to every corner of the fenced yard. There were so many little creatures that I could chase and tons of new smells that I could not identify.

It was really fun but then I discovered a hole in their fence. This was my chance at freedom again, so I wiggled through the hole and I was outta there.

I was about half way down the block when they caught up with me. I could have kept running but I figured it was best to get back to my puppies.

"You see...she just doesn't like us. She is a stray from the streets and that's where she wants to be." Sweetie said to Ann.

"Well, maybe you're right. I don't think she dislikes us but she doesn't seem to be really warming up to us either. I guess we should take her back and tell Karl that it just isn't going to work out." Ann said.

I could tell on the drive back that Ann was really sad. She kept petting me and I was trying to give her my sweetest face but I don't think she got it. Ray was pretty quiet but he just kept looking at me and Ann.

They started talking about their other dog named Max that had died. It sounded like they didn't want to get me because they were still so sad. I felt pretty rotten that I hadn't been nicer to her.

When I got back to my puppies, they were so happy to see me. I was happy to see them too but they are getting old enough to start eating big dog food and I know they won't be needing me much anymore. My job as their Mommy is to help them get ready to be good pets for the people that would adopt them.

I will miss them when they go to their new homes but it will also be nice and fun to have my freedom again. I think I have done a good job being a mother.

I had been so busy saying hello to my puppies that I almost missed Ann as she was leaving. When I saw her headed for the front door I ran really fast and jumped up on her and tried to let her know that I really did like her. You know, she was really nice to me and seemed pretty lonely. Maybe I should give these people a chance. I started licking her and wagging my tail and it made her so happy.

"You see, sweetie, she really does like us. Please let's think about keeping her. We still have a couple of weeks before her puppies are adopted." She said to sweetie.

"Okay, but I don't think it was us that she was running for. I think she was trying to escape when you opened the front door. But, we will talk about it some more when we get home and let Karl know what we decide." Sweetie said. "Thank you for letting us have her for the day."

A couple of weeks went by and Ann and sweetie came back. I heard her calling him Ray so that must be the name she uses after she gets what she wants.

She must have convinced him that they couldn't live without me and I think maybe I might like this idea of having a home. I am going to give it a shot and if it doesn't work I am pretty good at escaping. But for now, I think I am going to let them care for me. I think they need that right now.

Chapter 3

FIRST FRUIT OF THE SPIRIT
LOVE

It's been pretty easy getting settled into my new home. Ann and Ray seem quite eager to please me and they give me food and water two times a day. I love the backyard with so many birds, squirrels, and lizards to play with. They seem to like this game of chase that I play with them.

Ray has named me Sandy which is certainly better than "Dog". He said I was the color of the sand at the ocean so the name seemed to fit. Now I just need to find out what sand is.

Yesterday there was a bunny rabbit that ran through the yard. I chased it right through one of the holes in the fence.

"This rabbit can run really fast" I thought, but I managed to keep up. All of a sudden, it disappeared into a hole.

Ah ha! I got her." I thought but when I started to dig up the hole, I smelled the new baby bunny smell. I knew that this rabbit must have just had babies. I just couldn't keep digging since I knew she needed to take care of them. It wasn't that long ago that I had been in that same situation.

When I got back home, I couldn't find the hole I had escaped from so I started barking at the front door. When Ann opened it she was shocked to see me standing there.

"How did you get out here, you little rascal? What am I going to do with you? You can't just keep running away. You could get hit by a car." She was not at all happy with me but that didn't keep her from petting me.

I became more clever in my escaping techniques. The yard had a fence but there were so many ways to get out that it was hard to choose.

My favorite way out took me to Mr. Miners back yard. It was like a jungle with endless places to explore. He was rarely outside but when he was I discovered quickly that he did not like dogs at all.

On our first encounter, he threw a shoe at me and started screaming. "Get out of here you little mongrel. I don't want to have to start cleaning up after you too. These guinea pigs are bad enough." I wasn't sure what a guinea pig was but that would need to wait until later. Right now I need to get out of here. When I got back to the yard, Ann was outside looking for me. She didn't even know that I had been out of the yard.

Ann would spend time cuddling with me every morning. She would whisper in my ear, "I love you Sandy" over and over again. I didn't understand what that word meant but I could surely feel that overwhelming feeling that she had and also I started feeling the same way. I guess that is what she meant by the word "Love". It was probably the most special feeling that I have ever felt.

Ray was not as cuddly but he would play with me at night when it was time for bed. I would run into their room and jump on the bed with my toy just before they came in. He knew that it was playtime and we loved playing tug of war together.

When he was tired of playing, he'd pat me on my head to say goodnight. I could feel that same feeling of "love" from him too. He just showed it in a different way.

Life is pretty good at this place. In fact, I have a hard time remembering when I lived on the street or the people that abandoned me. I am just too happy to even think about that. Life is good now. And this feeling called "Love" just makes me feel good all over.

Chapter 4

SECOND FRUIT OF THE SPIRIT
JOY

So now that I am certain that this is my home and this is my new family, life has taken on a whole new meaning. I know what it feels like to be loved and I am starting to learn how to show love as well.

Mostly all I need to do to show them love is to let them love me. I have never had to share these feelings with anyone before so it is a learning process.

I have learned that it makes them very happy to greet them at the door with my tail wagging and my whole body wiggling. Ann seems to really like this a lot and she will even get down on the floor with me and give me an extra special tummy rub. If I am happy and having fun, then that is what makes them the happiest.

There is another feeling that love makes in my heart and that is joy. "Joy" fills my heart up just as much as "Love" does but it makes me want to share it with others. It feels like I am just going to pop open if I don't show this joy to others. So I decided I would try to share this "Joy" with Mr. Miner.

I snuck very cautiously through the fence so I wouldn't get his attention. I could hear him on the other side of the yard talking to someone. I walked carefully through the bushes to a point where I could see him and there he was squatting down and petting these furry little creatures. That must be what a guinea pig is.

He was saying, "Why do you little guys have to make such a mess? You know I love you but this endless poop is just too much to keep up with."

Just when he was saying this, one of the guinea pigs saw me and started squealing and running in circles. This was my chance to see how fast they could run so off I went chasing them. We ran around the shed, up over the rock, around the whole yard and then they scooted under the house.

To my surprise, the grouchy Mr. Miner was laughing so hard that tears were running down his cheeks. "Come here you little one. That was just the laugh that I needed today. My little piggies are starting to get fat and that's just the kind of exercise that they need. Maybe it's not so bad if you come back and play with them." He patted me on the head and then went to check on his pigs.

So maybe I got to spread some of that joy to Mr. Miner too. It felt good to make someone laugh and feel that joy too, especially since I was having so much fun doing it.

Chapter 5

THIRD FRUIT OF THE SPIRIT
PEACE

Most of my time is spent at our home but whenever we go for walks and have an encounter with another dog, it usually ends up with me barking and growling. Part of that is my duty to protect my new owners but the other part is fear that they will come after me the way those dogs did back in Oklahoma.

Ray and Ann have been trying to help me get better. When we are taking walks they will keep me close by their side on the leash and say, "Heal Sandy" as we are approaching another dog.

Most of the time, I will do pretty good even though my heart starts beating really fast and I'm ready to pounce if the other dog doesn't behave. But one day, this dog ran at me out of nowhere and starting biting me on my hind legs. This was a very big dog with brown and black hair and he was fast.

Ann was walking me that day and she started screaming and kicking the dog away. She was so mad and scared. I thought she was going to attack the dog herself but the owner finally came running out of the house and called his dog back into their yard.

I have never seen this side of Ann...she was so upset. "What is your dog doing out of the yard?" she said to the owner of the attack dog. "Don't you know that your dog can't run loose like this?"

"Well, your dog must have been in our yard" the man responded.

"We were just walking down the street and your dog just ran out of your yard and started biting Sandy. We did nothing to provoke him. I would suggest making sure your dog is going to be restrained in some way or I will need to let the city know. This is just not acceptable." Ann added.

The man just turned and walked away and we rushed home to see if I was bleeding. When we got there Ann was crying. She very carefully checked my back legs and there were several wounds and I was pretty sore.

"We better get you to the vet" she said. "I need to make sure you have all your shots."

After making a phone call, Ann picked me up and held me real close for a very long time. She stayed with me until we were both breathing more peacefully. I guess this was the first time I felt what "Peace" felt like. It was a very secure feeling and very relaxing. I felt so calm that I fell fast asleep right there in her arms.

Chapter 6

FOURTH FRUIT OF THE SPIRIT
PATIENCE

When I woke up, we were in this new place that had a million different animal smells; scared animals. Animals put off a certain smell when we are afraid.

We sat down in this room with people sitting and holding their pets. Everyone was waiting for something but I didn't know what they were waiting for. I felt pretty certain that it wasn't good with all this smell of fear.

Just when I was having that thought this lady wearing a white coat called my name. "Sandy, let's get you up on this scale to see how much you weigh" she said.

She took me across the room and put me on this little platform. This must be the scale she was talking about.

"Okay, that's it, 16 pounds and what a little cutie you are. What kind of puppy are you?"

Hum...now that's a question I have never heard before. I am a dog, plain and simple. What could she mean by "what kind"?

She led me into another smaller room with more of the "fear" smell. I wonder what happens in this little room?

After more waiting a man came in and he squatted down and began to pet me. He seemed really nice but I was still smelling all that fear so I decided not to wiggle or wag my tail.

"You are a cute little fella" he said.

"He is a she" said Ann. He laughed and said, "Well, she is certainly cute. It looks like she has some terrier in her and maybe a little Shih Tzu too. Let's get her up on the table and take a look at her."

I didn't know what all those words meant and I really didn't care to find out. I just wanted to get out of there as quickly as possible.

"We don't know much about her, not even how old she is. We came in today because she was attacked by our neighbors dog and it looks like she has some wounds on her back legs." Ann said.

"All right girl, let's take a look." He began to feel around on my back legs and I started to whine because it was really sore. "It looks like a few puncture wounds but nothing is broken. I want to make sure she gets her shots just to be on the safe side. I'll also clean out these wounds to make sure they don't get infected."

He stuck something real sharp in my hip but it didn't hurt too much but my wounds were burning after they put medicine on them.

"Now that wasn't too bad was it little girl?" He said. "You now have had your first shot."

I had never been to a place where they hurt you on purpose but Ann seems to be happy so I can't quite figure this out.

"How old do you think she is?" Ann inquired.

The man lifted up my jowl and looked at my teeth. "She's probably only a year old. It must have been during her first heat that she had her pups. Would you like her to have more puppies?" he asked. "I haven't really thought about it but I will let you know." Ann replied.

The man left the room for a long time and when he returned they started talking but by this time I was so exhausted from all of this fear and waiting around that I jumped down and sat next to the door and started whining again.

Ann said, "Sandy, you must be patient. We need to get all of this done so we can make sure you will be healthy."

More words that I didn't understand. "Healthy and patient." As I laid down on the floor next to the door I figured that this thing she called "patience" was something that I should learn. I think it means to slow down and wait without complaining or getting upset or angry. This must be a good thing since I really couldn't do anything about it anyway. I guess this wasn't so bad after all.

Later that day, Ann told me that patience is a Godly virtue and if you show patience for someone, then you are doing something that pleases God.

It has certainly been a long day and I realized that I hadn't seen Mr. Miner or the piggies in a few days. It was so much fun sharing that joy with him that I thought he might like to learn about peace and patience too.

After we got home and Ann got busy in the house I creeped under the fence again to see what might be happening.

Once I was close to Mr. Miners back door I heard him crying. Dogs know what to do when someone is sad. Since we can't talk, we don't ask a lot of questions or say something to make them feel better. We just know that if we sit real close to them and let them pet us, they will feel that peaceful feeling.

"You know how much I am hurting, don't you little girl." he said while patting me on my head. "I just can't get over this feeling of loneliness from loosing my dear friend."

I really didn't know when I came over here today that he was going to need me to patiently sit with him and give him my peace. I guess that God must have known and that's why He had me learn those lessons today so I could be ready to help Mr. Miner.

Chapter 7

FIFTH FRUIT OF THE SPIRIT
KINDNESS

Ray and Ann live alone but sometimes these wonderful playful children come over to visit.

The first time that I met them they all sat down and loved me and then started running around and squealing. I finally figured out that I was supposed to chase them. This was a fun game and since I was pretty used to chasing squirrels and the piggies, I was really good at chasing the children too.

They play with me a lot more than Ray and Ann. When they leave to go home I am always sad. It would be nice to have them to play with all the time.

Sometimes we go over to their house and the first time was not fun at all. They have two dogs named Penny and Polly. When I jumped out the car they started barking and growling. The adults were screaming and trying to pick us up so no one would get hurt. I wasn't biting but Ann didn't know that and was upset.

"Sandy, I told you that you shouldn't act like that with other dogs," she said. "But are you okay? We will need to slow down and let you get to know one another." And then she carried me into the house.

While being held, they allowed us to smell each others noses. I found out that these dogs are called chihuahua's and boy oh boy, can they bark.

After about 20 minutes of barking and sniffing each others noses and other parts, they let us down on the floor.

I was so tired of being held that I ran over to their back door so I could get outside away from all that barking.

We went down to the beach and that's when I understood why they named me Sandy. My fur looked just like the sand.

We had so much fun running and playing and getting that sand all over us. This place doesn't have any squirrels or lizards but it has these other wonderful creatures called dead fish that I love rolling in. Ann doesn't seem to like it when I do that but it makes me smell heavenly.

The girl named Cora decided to put sand all over me to see if it really matched my color. She seemed to think that was lots of fun, so I just laid there and let her do it. I love this place and I do hope we can come back here more often. Too bad Penny and Polly missed all the fun today but maybe next time they will go with us.

As time went on, Penny, Polly and I didn't fight anymore and actually started to like each other. They were really quite kind to me after a while and I started learning that when someone shows you kindness, it is really easy to show kindness back. Kindness means to be friendly, generous and considerate.

When I think back on when I first met Mr. Miner, he wasn't very kind to me since he threw that shoe at me but as time went by and I showed him my kindness, he started to be kind to me. I am slowly but surely learning to be a kinder dog. One kind word can change someone's entire day.

Chapter 8

SIXTH FRUIT OF THE SPIRIT
GOODNESS

Ann thought that if I was around more dogs, I wouldn't be so aggressive. She took me to a place that had lots and lots of dogs. More dogs than I had ever seen in one place before. They were all shapes and sizes, some nice and some mean but they all had one thing in common.... they all barked.

It seemed like the thing to do so I started barking too and every once in a while I would throw in a growl so I would sound tough.

I was so busy barking I didn't notice that a man had put a leash on me and was pulling me away from Ann. "Don't let them take me away, please, please." I barked.

Of course, she didn't understand me but she said, "Oh Sandy, don't worry, sweetie, they are going to take very good care of you." She looked terribly sad as she encouraged me to go along with this person.

He led me down a long hall and then put me in a big fenced yard with a lot of dogs. I didn't know what to do. I froze for a moment then did what I usually do, started growling and showing them how mean I was so they would not attack me.

Most of them ran away but one little white dog just stood there looking at me. I barked and growled some more but this dog just sat there looking at me with her head tilted to the side. She just wasn't getting mad or upset so I decided to stop and do a little sniffing.

When I approached her she just sat there and started to wag her tail. I let out another short growl but it didn't seem to frighten her so I figured this was a good sign.

I got in my "lets play" pose... with my front paws down and rear end up...and that's all it took. We were off and running and having the best time trying to take each other down.

Every once in a while she would walk over to me and lick my ears and just sit real close. I think she knew that I was just scared and all that growling was just for show. I felt this real good feeling in my heart and stomach. This dog was just a good dog. Not only was she kind but she had a good heart and wanted me to see that goodness.

I wondered if I had goodness in my heart. "Is that something you are born with or something that you learn?" I wondered. I wasn't sure which one it was but I knew that I wanted to be good.

Chapter 9

SEVENTH FRUIT OF THE SPIRIT
FAITHFULNESS

Ray and Ann both came to get me later in the day and I was dead tired from all that playing. I really didn't want to leave my new friend, whose name I found out was Nevaeh, (heaven spelled backward) but all I wanted to do was go home to my own house and my wonderful backyard and just sleep. Not even food could tempt me to stay awake.

On the ride home I began to consider all that I had learned since coming to Florida and my new home. I didn't even know there were feelings like this. I felt like I belonged and that I was loved and would be cared for.

This journey that I have been on has certainly been interesting and it all started with Karl showing me kindness. Karl was so faithful to stand by me through all the trials of getting my puppies and me a new home.

It seems like all of these things go hand and hand. If you are kind and show people love then they will probably be the same way to you. Ann said that is the "Golden Rule". Treat other people the way you want them to treat you.

Ray and Ann have also been so faithful to me through all of my barking and attacking dogs. I think that I will love them forever and ever.

I hope to show them that I will be a faithful dog and will always be at their sides to protect them and show them the same love. These lessons don't come so easily to a dog that has lived on the streets but I sure do like the way I feel.

Oh....in case you were wondering what happened to my puppies Bootsie, Mopsie and Skully; they all got adopted by 3 great families who are all friends so they get to play together all the time. I even get to see them every so often too.

Chapter 10

EIGHTH FRUIT OF THE SPIRIT
GENTLENESS

Ann woke me up this morning and said we were going on a weekend adventure. Sounded good to me since now I know that adventures are not only fun but you also learn so much when you do things you are a little afraid of doing.

We got into this giant car that they called a motorhome and started driving. It made me quite nervous so I decided I better sit on Ann's lap and watch Ray drive. This thing was huge and I wanted to make sure he was being careful. Sometimes he would hit the bumps on the side of the road and it made an awful noise. That was my cue to bark and make sure he was paying attention. Since he was doing a pretty good job, I decided to take a nap so I would be ready to go and play when we arrived.

When we stopped, Ray and Ann started setting things up outside and building a campfire. They got so busy that they must have forgotten that I was with them so I used that opportunity to do a little exploring.

We were surrounded by trees and before I knew it I was deep in the middle of them. I looked up ahead and there was a bunny rabbit just sitting there looking at me. I stopped and got in my stalking position where I don't move a muscle. We were eye to eye and he seemed paralyzed so I decided to move very slowly in my stealth mode. I got about two steps and he took off running.

I was so excited because chasing creatures is just about my favorite thing in life. We ran through ditches, over fallen logs, down hills, next to the lake and I just couldn't keep up. As I ran up a hill and got to the top, he just disappeared. I found a hole that smelled like a bunny but I was to big to get inside. I guess he won that race.

When I looked around, I realized I had no idea how to get back to where Ray and Ann were. I got a little panicked and started running. I was going so fast I didn't notice the patch of stickers and ran right into them. I had them in all four of my paws and it was so painful to walk.

It was getting late and I was getting scared that I might never find them again. Just then I heard Ann's voice. " Sandy, Sandy, where are you little girl. Come Sandy!" Then she would whistle. I started barking as loud as I could and in just a few minutes, there she was standing over me.

"Oh my goodness, what have you gotten yourself into this time?" Ann said. She started yelling for Ray and saying she had found me. "When will you ever learn to stay close to us so that we can protect you?"

She picked me up and ever so gently started pulling the stickers out of my paws. It would hurt just for a second when they came out but then it felt so good to have them gone. She was so tender and gentle as she did this that after a while it didn't hurt at all.

I started licking my paws to help them to heal and felt Ann and Ray's gentle touch. It's not that they hadn't been gentle before but I guess I had never thought about "gentleness".

It's a combination of being kind and tender and I was certainly glad that Ann was so good at it. Now I will need to remember to show gentleness to others.

I thought about how when my puppies were little and I would play roughly with them. They would yelp because I guess I just didn't understand about gentleness. No one had ever been gentle with me before.

If I ever catch one of those bunnies or squirrels, maybe I can show them gentleness too.

Chapter 11

NINETH FRUITS OF THE SPIRIT
SELF CONTROL

I have been in my new home for almost a year now and we have all settled into our routine.

Mornings are pretty lazy with Ray and Ann having their coffee and reading their Bibles while I slowly make my way over to the backdoor to start scouting for where the squirrels are hiding today.

I have found that if I sit real still the squirrels will come right up to the door and not even see me. Sometimes I start to shake because I am so tempted to bark and go crazy. I learned that when I do that, the squirrels would just run away and hide. By controlling my barking and desire to run after them, I have learned that I get to chase them so much farther.

It takes a lot of self control to keep from barking and being too eager to get out there and start hunting but with patience and self control I get to have much more fun.

Soon it's time for our morning walk and then time for a romp around the backyard to give the squirrels their exercise. Can't have them getting lazy.

In the afternoon, we will take another walk around the block but sometimes we drive to the beach and walk there.

Boy oh boy is that fun. The beach has this soft ground that squeezes between my toes and I can run really fast. What makes it even more fun is having the kids there.

Today is Sunday and that's usually a pretty lazy day. I was thinking about all those things that I have learned, like love, joy, peace, patience, kindness, goodness, faithfulness and gentleness. They all start with love and then kind of build on each other.

You get the joy and peace from knowing how to love and trust. Once you know how to do those then you develop the patience you need to show the next four things.

Kindness is something that you show to others and goodness is something that you have inside of you so you can show that kindness.

Once you have the goodness in your heart then you become gentle and that leads to being faithful. I learned how to be faithful from Ray and Ann. They were always there for me so I wanted to be the same for them.

The last thing I learned is self control and that has been the hardest one so far. I still like to do what I want to do but I have learned that what I want isn't always what is best for me.

Doing what is right is always the best decision and it takes self control to say "no" to something that I want.

In time, I have learned that if I can control myself and trust Ray and Ann to lead me in the right direction, I know ultimately that I will be the happiest.

Another word for saved is rescued and that is what Ann, Ray and Karl did for me.

I can't wait to tell you about how I became known as "Huntin' Dog" and to take you on our many adventures around our beautiful country.

But for now.....I'll say goodbye.

Chapter 12

SUMMING IT UP

You may be wondering how a dog got smart enough to learn all these things. Well, first of all, dogs are much smarter than you think they are. The more you communicate with us, the more we understand.

I heard Ann reading one day from a man named David Jeremiah. He wrote, "Maturity takes time; the fruit of the Spirit is evidence of God's conforming us to the image of Christ. Today's weakness can be tomorrow's strength."

That makes a lot of sense to me. When Karl found me, all I had were my puppies. I didn't understand much about anything since there was no one to teach me. Boy am I grateful that I was rescued by such a kind and gentle man. Even though he couldn't keep me, he made sure to find the right home for me. He calls me his "God dog".

Ray and Ann have taught me all the fruits of the spirit and so much more but I think that I have taught them something too, God's unconditional love. I will love them forever; no matter what.

Another man named Erwin W. Lutzer said "There are no shortcuts to spiritual maturity. It takes time to be holy." I don't know if a dog can ever be considered holy but remember that GOD spelled backwards is DOG.